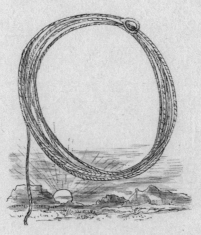

PRAISE FOR
Basil in the Wild West

"A welcome new mystery for
detective story fans."
—*Booklist*

"Titus keeps the action brisk, skillfully
combining suspense with tongue-in-cheek
humor, and Galdone's humorous line
drawings add just the right accent."
—*School Library Journal*

READ MORE ABOUT

Basil's adventures!

Basil of Baker Street
Basil and the Cave of Cats
Basil in Mexico

COMING SOON

Basil and the Lost Colony

THE
GREAT MOUSE
DETECTIVE
Basil in the Wild West

BY *Eve Titus*

ILLUSTRATED BY *Paul Galdone*

ALADDIN WITHDRAWN

NEW YORK LONDON TORONTO SYDNEY NEW DELHI

This book is a work of fiction. Any references to historical events, real people, or real places are used fictitiously. Other names, characters, places, and events are products of the author's imagination, and any resemblance to actual events or places or persons, living or dead, is entirely coincidental.

ALADDIN

An imprint of Simon & Schuster Children's Publishing Division
1230 Avenue of the Americas, New York, New York 10020
This Aladdin paperback edition February 2017
Text copyright © 1982 by Eve Titus
Cover illustration copyright © 2017 by David Mottram
Interior illustrations copyright © 1982 by Paul Galdone
Also available in an Aladdin hardcover edition.
All rights reserved, including the right of reproduction in whole or in part in any form.
ALADDIN and related logo are registered trademarks of Simon & Schuster, Inc.
For information about special discounts for bulk purchases, please contact
Simon & Schuster Special Sales at 1-866-506-1949 or business@simonandschuster.com.
The Simon & Schuster Speakers Bureau can bring authors to your live event.
For more information or to book an event contact the Simon & Schuster
Speakers Bureau at 1-866-248-3049 or visit our website at www.simonspeakers.com.
Cover designed by Karin Paprocki
Interior designed by Mike Rosamilia
The text of this book was set in Perpetua.
Manufactured in the United States of America 0117 OFF
2 4 6 8 10 9 7 5 3 1
Library of Congress Control Number 2016948050
ISBN 978-1-4814-6411-6 (hc)
ISBN 978-1-4814-6410-9 (pbk)
ISBN 978-1-4814-6412-3 (eBook)

For Jane Trevarthen Traub's
wonderful research center
Book Bridge
(where one may browse in any language)

Cast of Characters

BASIL OF BAKER STREET	*a British mouse detective*
DR. DAVID Q. DAWSON	*his friend and associate*
FRANCO CELADA	*border police chief*
TERESA	*his worried wife*
LONGFELLOW	*a pony, founder of CLOPS*
VERDI	*his grandson*
TOM TALLTREES	*an Indian mouse*
WENONAH	*his bride*
J.J.	*master smuggler*
PETE BLAU	*his aide*
BENNETT SHAW	*a mouse sheriff*
COLONEL GILLEN	*a military mouse*
THE THING	*?????????*
IVY AND IAN THORBRIDGE	*hotel owners*
PAT MARTIN, MIKE MULLEN	*hotel guards*
MONTEREY JACK	*a mouse outlaw leader*
GIDDY AND GABBY	*members of his gang*
KEATS, YEATS, ROSSINI, CHERUBINI, SPONTINI, PUCCINI, HUMPERDINCK	*CLOPS ponies*
AUGUST AND DEBORAH BERGER FATIMA DOMIATI OSMAN DURAK ALFRED AND LYNN GILMORE MARY ANN GOODE DONALD RICKSON THE COUNTESS	*Hathaway Hotel guests (alphabetically)*

(and Hundreds of Other Ponies and Mice!)

Contents

1

AT THE BORDER

PERCHED ON THE BACK OF A BURRO, BASIL AND I peered into the distance, paws shielding our eyes against the blazing sun.

"At long last—the Arizona border!" declared the detective. "I wonder what awaits us in the wild and wonderful West."

He stroked the burro's shaggy neck. "Here we part. A thousand thanks for transporting us from Mexico City. You'll be missed!"

"Greatly missed, dear Carmencita," said I.

She turned her head to regard us fondly. Tiny tears glistened in her large brown eyes.

"I'll miss you both. Never have I carried

passengers so famous—Basil of Baker Street, the Sherlock Holmes of the Mouse World! And you, Dr. Dawson, author of the books about Basil, the world's best detective."

"Second best, my dear burro," said the sleuth. "Mr. Holmes is first. I study at his feet in Baker Street. But here's someone to inspect our passports and luggage. Will you kneel?"

Long ears flopping, she knelt, waited 'til we'd scurried down, then smiled and left us.

As she jogged southward, I recalled our exciting Mexican adventures. . . .

I, Dr. David Q. Dawson, am a medical mouse. Basil and I share lodgings in the cellar of Baker Street, 221B, where dwell Mr. Sherlock Holmes and Dr. Watson. Tall and lean, with a hawklike profile, Basil resembles his hero as much as a mouse may resemble a man.

We'd gone overseas to Mexico in 1895. A famous painting, the *Mousa Lisa,* had been stolen. Basil tracked down the thief and the masterpiece.

Then I was held hostage by El Bruto and Professor Ratigan, Basil's long-time enemy, who tried to rule the mice of Mexico. Basil rescued me, and had the criminals put in prison.

Lord Hathaway, British Mouse Ambassador to Mexico, asked Basil to investigate a mystery at a mouse hotel in the Grand Canyon, owned by the Thorbridges, his former cook and butler. Basil had agreed to take the case.

And now, near Arizona, we were meeting

Chief Celada, of the Mexican border policemice. He was also head customs officer, examining all goods brought into or taken out of Mexico.

(By the way, during the events narrated on these pages, I kept expecting Ratigan, an escape artist, to appear, seeking revenge. But he stayed safely behind bars, and the cases in this book deal only with American criminals.)

Celada recognized us at once, and led us to his rambling Spanish-style home nearby.

"*Es su casa!* My house is yours! Please be our guests overnight. After so many nights on the road, you must be weary indeed."

We accepted. After dinner, Mrs. Celada served a tray of many cheeses—Asadero from Mexico, Lipto from Hungary, Feta from Greece, Domiati from Egypt, Asiago from Italy, Bleu from France, Anatolian from Turkey, and others.

Nibbling Camembert, Basil said the Emperor Napoleon had named it, after the tiny town of Camembert where he'd first tasted it, and had even kissed the waitress who'd served him.

We next discussed crime, and I asked Celada whether any smuggling went on.

He sighed deeply. "I know that smugglers operate constantly, smiling all the while, but I haven't a shred of proof! All along the border from Texas to New Mexico to Arizona to California we search and question mice, but haven't captured a single smuggler. They've made fools of all the border policemice! You see, in Mexico, objects long buried beneath the soil are often discovered. Some are hundreds of years old, and are valuable antiquities. It is against Mexican law to remove these originals from our country. Yet I hear that outside our land dishonest collectors are buying our ancient relics from the head of a huge smuggling ring."

Basil sat erect, eyes agleam. "Chief, I've not used my wits on a case in weeks. My brain may be rusting away! Pray tell me about the Case of the Smiling Smugglers."

"Teresa, please give Basil some of the background," said Celada. "I'll chime in later."

We sat back to listen.

2

THE CASE OF THE
SMILING SMUGGLERS

"IN MEXICO," BEGAN TERESA, "MOUSE SCIENTISTS are always on the lookout for priceless old originals that are part of our proud heritage. We call these objects pre-Columbian, for they existed long before Columbus discovered America. Sometimes they're found by chance. A farmer, for instance, while plowing his land, may come upon an object centuries old. He stops plowing and notifies the Mousmopolitan, our government museum. Experts go out to the farm. They dig carefully, so as not to damage the valuable find, and carry it off to the museum, after paying the farmer a small finder's fee. But alas, many priceless pieces are smuggled out of Mexico by criminals!"

Basil interrupted. "No doubt a brainy boss plans all their operations. Tell me, what types of mice cross your borders?"

The Chief answered, "All types! Mexicans working or studying in the United States, North Americans studying in Mexico, tourists from all over the world. These visitors help business. Our hotels and restaurants are crowded with foreigners. Souvenir shops sell them thousands of souvenirs daily. We welcome them all, but—*which ones are smugglers?* I've become jumpy, moody, nervous. My reputation's at stake, and these smiling smugglers may cost me my job!"

I looked at Celada and said, "I'd prescribe a tonic, but your raggedy nerves stem from this smuggling situation, for which, unluckily, I have no remedy."

"Ah, but *I* have!" cried Basil. "Mr. Holmes' method, and mine, is to observe, to analyze, to deduce. A Japanese saying—*to know the unknowable, to seek the unseekable*—best describes the art of scientific sleuthing."

He paused. "Chief, the Case of the Smiling Smugglers is already ninety percent solved."

"It *is?*" cried our astonished hosts.

"Bravo, Basil!" said I. "You're like a magician pulling a rabbit out of a hat. But then, you always solve cases quickly when you play the role of armchair detective."

"What's an armchair detective?" asked Celada.

I winked at Basil, then bowed low.

"Forsooth, O, Sleuth, be not uncouth! Explain in words that ring of truth."

He groaned. "You're a bad poet, but you don't know it. Stick to doctoring, Dawson!"

He faced the Celadas. "I shall explain."

ARMCHAIR
DETECTIVE

"WHEN A DETECTIVE IS CALLED IN ON A CASE," began Basil, "he is told what has happened so far. Usually he goes to the scene of the crime, seeking clues. He uses equipment such as his magnifying lens, measuring devices, etc. He questions suspects, scans local newspapers, and listens to all the neighborhood gossip. He is aware that one tiny fact, just like a jigsaw puzzle piece, may fit into another tiny fact to make the entire picture crystal clear.

"But sometimes the facts told to him at the start arrange themselves so logically in his mind that the bits and pieces fall into place at once. Without even leaving his armchair, the detective solves the case. This has just occurred, because you presented the facts so clearly, and I thank you both."

He yawned. "Time to head for bed, Dawson."

"*Please* don't leave us in suspense," I cried. "Basil, I beg you to tell us more!"

"Basil, I beseech you!" cried Celada.

"Basil, I entreat you!" cried Teresa.

"Very well, then. Picture a mouse farmer whom we'll call Carlos. He earns barely enough to keep his wife and six children from starving.

"One day a smiling stranger appears, gives the children lemon drops and lollipops, and tells the farmer that he brings good news.

"Inside the house he says, 'I hear that you plowed up a statue six hundred years old.'

"'*Si, señor.* I stopped plowing and notified the government museum. Experts came to dig it up. They paid me and took the statue away.'

"'How many pesos were you paid?' asked the stranger, and when told, puts on a sad face.

"'Alas, you weren't paid enough! I work for the rich owners of a new museum. They would have paid you twice as much! We collect ancient art, and many farmers sell what they find to us instead of to the government, because we pay more.'

"'But I was told that the government should have first choice,' declares Carlos.

"'Bah! Promise to deal with us and we'll pay you some money in advance, right now.'

"The children never have enough to eat, and need new clothes, so Carlos and his wife agree. The stranger pays them some money and leaves."

Basil rose, began pacing to and fro.

"Carlos and the other farmers don't know that they've been fooled. The story about the museum is an out-and-out lie—the museum doesn't exist! These smiling strangers, who are the smugglers' agents, keep on persuading Mexican farmers to sell them valuable pre-Columbian relics found in the soil. The pieces are then smuggled into the U.S.A., and sent to the head of the ring, who probably lives in a southwestern state. Dishonest collectors visit him. Aware that they're buying illegally, they pay sky-high prices and ask no questions."

"But Basil, I still don't understand," said Celada. "Just how is the smuggling done?"

"You gave me my clue when you mentioned the souvenirs. Year after year, the bestselling and most popular items in souvenir shops are copies of originals. Everybody brings them back home. Your clever criminals pretend the originals they carry are copies. What mice on your staff are expert enough to distinguish a copy from an original? None, I'll wager!"

"Correct. We're border police, and good ones, but know nothing about museum pieces. What do you advise me to do, Basil?"

"Add experts to your staff. If museum mice at the border examine all so-called copies, the smiling smugglers will soon stop smiling!"

"And that's when *I'll* start smiling again," said Celada happily. "I'll expand my staff as soon as possible, with experts from the Mousmopolitan Museum. Basil, for what you've done, I thank you from the bottom of my heart! You've made a new mouse of me!"

"Perhaps he'll stop losing weight now," said Teresa. "Because of the smugglers, my husband has lost more ounces than I care to count."

"I have a suggestion," said Celada. "Basil, why not work with me at the border tomorrow? You're an expert—we'll catch a few smugglers."

"Capital!" cried the sleuth. "One of them may squeal if offered a shorter jail term for turning informer. If we learn where the head of the ring is, we'll wire the Sheriff there to move in and arrest Mr. Big. By the way, Chief, how do Dawson and I travel to Grand Canyon?"

"You'll go via CLOPS," replied Celada. "You look a bit puzzled, *amigos*. Therefore, I shall let Teresa enlighten you."

4
THE STORY
OF CLOPS

TERESA'S TALE STARTED WITH HORACE GREELEY'S famous words, *"Go West, Young Man, Go West!'* Thousands of young men heeded those words. Then, upon spying a mouse in her house, Mrs. Greeley said, *'Go West, Young Mouse, Go West!'* Her words were also heeded, and many mice stowed away in railway cars and wagon trains.

"The wee pioneers loved the West, but vast distances between towns kept them from visiting friends and relatives elsewhere. There were trains, but hiking miles to a station under a hot sun was too tiring for most mice.

"Herds of wild ponies roamed the West, running free as the wind. Proud and untamed, they lived in hidden secret canyons unknown to men.

"Often these friendly ponies visited mouse towns. We'd give them lumps of sugar, and they'd offer lifts to mice going their way.

"One day a mousewife named Melissa offered a pony cheese. He adored it, told the others, and cheese became their favorite food.

"The ponies loved poetry and music, and were named for poets and musicians. Longfellow, their leader, came up with a wonderful idea. He asked our carpenters to make ponycarts for ten or more

mice, and howdahs, covered platforms people use when riding elephants, for less than ten travelers. In return for whatever cheese we could spare, ponies would make regular stops at our towns, and transport us all over the West.

"Thus was CLOPS founded, years ago. CLOPS stands for Cheese Lovers Official Pony Service. Longfellow's a grandfather now, but still active, and due here day after tomorrow. He'll gladly transport you both. And so ends my tale, or should I say—my ponytail?"

We thanked our hosts, and went off to bed.

Next day at the border Basil and the Chief questioned all mice crossing into the U.S.A. Some had copies of ancient art, as they claimed. Others lied. With his magnifying lens, Basil detected which were copies and which were the real thing. Several mice were arrested, but none would turn informer.

Then a handsome student came, bearing books and a small box with two stone statuettes.

Flashing a big smile, he said, "I know the statuettes look old, but they're just cheap copies I picked up at a souvenir shop."

Basil held up his lens. "This will tell me whether you speak falsely. Copies, you say?"

The big smile gave way to a worried frown.

Basil examined the statuettes, then said sternly, "They're originals! It's against the law to remove them from Mexico. You're under arrest for trying to smuggle them through."

The student shook like a leaf. "Sir, I've never smuggled before. My mother's a hardworking widow. It'll break her heart if I go to prison. Please give me another chance!"

"On one condition. Tell us the name of the head of the smuggling ring!"

"I don't know his name. A friend talked me into smuggling. He showed me a letter from the big boss, with instructions. But no name was signed, just the initials, *J.J.*"

"Do you recall nothing more?" asked Basil. "What was the postmark on the envelope?"

"It was postmarked Moriarty, New Mexico."

At that, my friend flew into a rage.

"Moriarty?" he roared, "MORIARTY? The monster of a man who hounds Sherlock Holmes, whose gangs wage constant war against the Great Detective? Who would name a town after that villain? Nobody! Surely you jest."

"Sorry, sir, it's true. I saw the postmark."

But Basil raved on. "The perfidious Professor Moriarty, brilliant but beastly! Rogue, ruffian, rotter, racketeer, reprobate, rat—"

"Be calm, control yourself!" I cried. "It's a different Moriarty! Stop shouting!"

He quieted down, but insisted on having the last word. "A town called after an evildoer? Only in America could this happen, never in England!

Dawson, I've changed my plans. We'll go to the Grand Canyon later, after we visit Moriarty, New Mexico. It will give me great satisfaction to jail this J.J. in a town named after Mr. Holmes' eternal enemy."

The student was freed, after some stern warnings, and we returned to Celada's home.

Longfellow, a charming old chap, came at dawn. He was a shaggy Shetland pony, with good legs and a full chest.

As he jogged along, we marveled at the breathtaking beauty of the American West.

We saw mountain peaks that seemed to touch the clouds, peaceful green valleys, and vast stretches of prairie. We saw gently rolling hills, cascading waterfalls, and tall cliffs jutting skyward. The rangeland seemed endless, and we rode up steep trails that led us into fairytale forests.

Fantastically shaped rocks and boulders were strewn across the land as though hurled from above by a giant hand. Some looked like cathedrals, or castles, some like great stone faces.

Basil and I kept arguing as to which was the loveliest, sunrise or sunset, until Longfellow wisely pointed out that such masterpieces of nature were best enjoyed in awed silence.

Riding through the desert was a new experience for us. The air was fresh and bracing. We had expected the desert to be monotonous and flat, but there were dunes and hills and cliffs of sand whose colors changed constantly in sun and in shadow.

Longfellow said the whirling winds of sandstorms had created them, and told us what to do should such a storm spring up. It was lucky that he

did, for the very next day a severe sandstorm struck!

Scurrying to the ground, we threw blankets over Longfellow's lowered head, then blanketed our own heads and clung to the pony's legs, lest we be blown away. So much sand swirled by, and with so much force, that sand particles stung our faces through the thick blankets.

Afterward, dislodging the gritty stuff from our teeth, we agreed that a sandstorm was one wonder of the West we'd never miss.

5

TOM TALLTREES

WE RODE ON, LEFT ARIZONA TERRITORY, AND entered New Mexico, heading north by northeast.

At night the red and orange flames of our campfire flickered cheerily. We would toast cheese on long sticks, and then Basil would play his flute. Many furred and feathered creatures listened to the melodies that soared high and clear in the wilderness.

An owl swooped down once, not to harm us, but to hear the music. She recognized the detective at once—his renown is worldwide.

She especially liked a piece he'd written himself, based on the poem, *The Owl and the Pussycat,* and said she'd pass the word to birds to leave us alone. We were thankful—far too many flyers find mice tasty.

After she left, Basil reached for his gun.

"On guard, Dawson! I hear a prowler."

"Who goes there?" he called. "Show yourself!"

Out of the darkness strode a tall, handsome Indian mouse, holding his paws high.

"Don't shoot! I come in peace. Whose sharp ears detected my presence out there?"

He spied Basil. "So the sharp ears belong to Basil of Baker Street! I'm Tom Talltrees."

Longfellow, who'd been dozing, looked up.

"Hello there, Tom. Sorry I missed the wedding—had a trip scheduled. Congratulations! How's the blushing bride, winsome Wenonah?"

"Fine, except for a sprained ankle. Heard you were going to Moriarty, near Palma, where we live. Any chance of a ride?"

"Of course. And the ankle will have Dr. Dawson's personal care. Where's your wife?"

Wenonah was nearby. I bound up the ankle, and told her she'd be riding with us.

Her lovely face brightened. "Good! Now we won't miss school. Tom and I are teachers."

Riding along, Tom told us about the mouse town of Moriarty, built in the deserted courtyard of a burnt-out building, a mile beyond the people's town of Moriarty. No humans ever bothered to visit the area, for a fire had made charred skeletons of all the buildings there.

"It's a bad town, Basil, owned lock, stock, and barrel by an evil mouse called J.J."

"My mission is to capture J.J.," said Basil.

"A difficult task. He owns more land than anyone else, has the biggest bank account. He's tough, hard as nails. When mice can't pay money they owe on their homes, and beg for more time, he sends his gangsters to throw the family off the land, furniture and all. Then he takes over. I hear that he plans to set up a superstate, and rule it as king, with life-and-death powers over all mice."

"Do many strangers visit him?" inquired Basil.

Tom nodded. "A renegade pony named Satan trots them off to J.J.'s ranch. They return with bulky packages. Nobody knows what's in the packages. Your guess is as good as mine."

The sleuth smiled. "No need to guess—I know.

J.J. heads a gigantic smuggling ring, operating out of Mexico. Tell me more, Tom."

Longfellow interrupted. "Lawless ponies *do* team up with mouse criminals, but there are few like Satan. My grandson Verdi worked for a seemingly honest mouse. When he learned his boss was a bank robber, Verdi told Mouse Sheriff Shaw about the next job that was planned. Shaw set up a trap. The holdup failed, the gang was jailed, and Verdi's more careful now."

"I'd like to meet Verdi," said Tom. "I hear he sings arias from every opera written by his namesake, the man Giuseppe Verdi. But about J.J.—I've never seen him. My friend Cactus Charlie has, says he's mean-looking, with piggish eyes and a very long tail he usually keeps across his lap. Charlie says it's easy to see J.J.'s smaller than average, even though he's always sitting down."

"Always sitting down? Why?" I asked.

"Heavens, Tom," cried Wenonah, "you forgot to tell them he's in a wheelchair. His bodyguards told Charlie that because of a bad fall, J.J. will never walk again."

"Then once we get past the guards," said the detective, "capturing him should be easy."

"Dead wrong, Basil. His ranch is like an armed fort. Guards with rifles patrol it day and night, inside and out. Any mouse approaching must know the password, or he's booted out, at gunpoint. High walls surround the ranch house patio, with barbed wire strung all along the tops of the walls."

"Nobody could possibly climb those walls," added Wenonah. "J.J. is devilishly clever! He had glue poured along the top, and sprinkled it thickly with broken glass."

Tom's eyes bored into Basil's. "I admire and respect you as a brilliant detective, but I must speak frankly. Your chances of capturing J.J. are practically zero. The obstacles are too many and too great. In my opinion, Basil, you're on an impossible mission!"

THE WALKING BUSHES

THERE WAS A STEELY LOOK IN THE DETECTIVE'S eyes as he faced Tom Talltrees.

I knew that look well. It meant he'd push on relentlessly against all odds. It meant he'd never falter, that nothing but death or destruction would swerve him from his goal.

His voice was grim as he answered Tom.

"Despite what you say, I refuse to give up! I have two goals. First, to deliver J.J. to Sheriff Bennett Shaw himself, in Moriarty. Second, to arrange for the stolen originals to go back to the Mexican museum. I'll not stop until I accomplish this. Do I make myself clear?"

Tom nodded, and Basil asked, "Do you know of a secret trail that leads to the ranch? If we go through Moriarty, J.J. will know we're coming. I'd rather surprise him."

"I salute your courage!" cried Tom. "There's an old trail that ends near the ranch. I'll guide you there. And, if you'll permit me, I'll do more than guide you—I'll join you as an ally. May I?"

We accepted. Now we'd be three against the criminals instead of two. Wenonah and Longfellow remained at the campsite while our newly formed trio raced along a forest trail.

We emerged on the edge of a cliff overlooking the ranch buildings. Unseen by those below, we lay flat on our stomachs, watching.

A pair of heavy doors in one of the walls led into the courtyard. Two guards were stationed outside the big doors, four inside.

Basil eyed the outside guards. While one stood at attention near the doors, the other patrolled a path winding to the foot of the cliff. There he about-faced and marched back to his partner at the doors. The two saluted, and then the other took his turn patrolling the path.

Basil rose. "I've decided upon my strategy," said he, descending a side of the cliff that faced away from the ranch. We followed. When we touched ground, the guards were back at the doors, saluting. Quickly Basil cut down a tall bush, and signalled us to do the same. Crouching behind the bush, he held it before him like a screen, and began inching forward. So did we.

Bushes that walked—what clever strategy! They concealed our bodies as we moved toward the path. When the guard faced our way, we froze, and were instantly invisible! He stared straight at us but saw us not, for those bushes camouflaged us completely!

The guard about-faced. At Basil's nod, Tom sprang, and bore the guard to the ground. After tying him up and gagging him with his own bandana, we hid him behind a rock. He glared at us with such hate-filled eyes that if looks could kill, we would have been three dead mice.

The walking bushes stood still as we waited for the other guard to come seeking his comrade.

"Johnny, Johnny Sohl!" he called. "Where'd you go, pal? Stop playin' games. C'mon out!"

He waited, then muttered, "Sure is mighty strange. Reckon I'd better tell Pete Blau."

When this guard about-faced, it was I who pounced. We trussed him up and laid him behind the rock, next to his partner.

Next came an important part of Basil's strategy. When he became a consulting detective, the stage lost a great actor. Let him hear a voice but once and he can mimic it perfectly.

We saw his lips moving, but out came the guard's own voice.

"Hey, Pete Blau! Johnny's plumb disappeared. Don't see him nowhere. What'll I do, Petey?"

The door opened halfway. A head poked out, a pair of eyes surveyed the scene. We waited behind our bushes, as still as statues.

"I can't see ya, Sy. Where are ya at?"

"Over by the cliff, Pete," answered Basil.

"Huntin' Johnny, are ya? Wait a sec. I'll send Bob and Mike and Barry to help ya look."

When they came, we played no favorites, but treated all three as we'd treated the others.

We celebrated our success in a weird way. The bushes walked, the bushes stalked, they hopped, skipped, and jumped, they danced, pranced, advanced, and did the Highland Fling!

But when Pete Blau peeped out, the bushes moved not at all. We hoped he'd step outside to seek his friends, but waited in vain—he didn't fall into our clutches.

"Blau's brainier than the rest," remarked Basil. "He's probably in the house, telling J.J. about the mystery of the missing guards."

We looked up at the darkening sky. Rain began to fall. It soon became a heavy downpour, soaking us to the fur. Streaks of lightning cut across the heavens, thunder rumbled ominously in the distance.

"We'll confront J.J.," said Basil. "Blau forgot to bolt the doors the last time he looked out. It's now or never—in we go!"

Thunder pealed as Basil kicked the doors open. Our guns at the ready, we edged inside.

MISSION—
IMPOSSIBLE???

PELTING RAIN HAD MUDDIED THE PATHWAY TO THE house. We sloshed through puddles. It was so dark that only when lightning flashed could we see the veranda and the doorway.

Suddenly the storm ended. The rays of the afternoon sun lent an unreal golden glow to the scene. Framed in the doorway was a figure in a wheelchair—the elusive J.J.!

Cactus Charlie had described him well, from piggish eyes to his cruel, mean expression. A robe covered his lower limbs, and his long tail lay curved across his lap.

The worst was over. We'd cornered him, yet I still felt uneasy. Was it a premonition?

His lips parted in a nasty snarl.

"Do my eyes deceive me? It's the snoopy sleuth of Baker Street, and two of his pals! I heard you were hot on my trail. You can be sure it's no pleasure to meet you!"

"No pleasure for us, either," replied Basil, "but we'll enjoy escorting you to jail. Shall Tom Talltrees wheel you there? Dr. Dawson? Myself? The choice is yours."

"Nobody throws *me* in the clink!" yelled J.J.

"My dear smuggler, you'll be tried for your crimes, and rot in prison. You can stop dreaming about ruling a kingdom of your own. In 1776 Americans refused to bow down to George the Third. Now, in 1895, they'd never put up with the tyrant J.J. the First. Or would you rather be called J.J. the Worst?"

"You'll pay for those insults! After I escape to my California hideout, my toughest gangmice will track you down. You'll suffer!"

Basil pretended to yawn. "My, my. By the way, what does J.J. stand for—Jailbird Jim? Jughead Jake? Jellybean Joe? Jesse James?"

J.J. smirked. "So you think you've got me dead to rights! Well, don't count chickens before they're hatched, and don't count criminals before they're catched!"

"Didn't you learn grammar at school?" teased Basil. "The word's *caught,* not *catched.*"

"Caught, catched—who gives a hoot? The point is, I'm smart enough to escape!"

What happened next was so unexpected that all three of us were struck speechless.

J.J. sprang from his wheelchair!

"Never needed the chair! Tried to nab me, eh? Out of my way, you defective detective!"

He zigzagged past us, swift as a deer!

We gave chase. I stumbled, fell flat on my face in the mud. Wiping the sticky stuff out of my eyes, I hoped the others had caught him, but to my surprise they stood nearby, looking dazed.

Basil, as though in a trance, was mumbling strange syllables. *"Zapodidae, Neozapus, Zapodidae, Neozapus, Zapodidae, Neozapus—"*

"Have you lost your wits?" I asked.

"Dawson, why didn't I deduce the truth? There were clues—his smaller size, the unusually long tail. *Zapodidae, Neozapus—*"

I turned to Tom, demanded, "Where's J.J.?"

He pointed to the sky, and I gazed upward.

To the west, outlined against an orange sun, a figure high in the air took a long leap forward, bounced back to earth, then leaped again and bounced back, moving farther and farther away.

I was puzzled. "A kangaroo? In New Mexico?"

"It's no kangaroo," said Tom. "It's J.J."

"You should remember your Latin, Dawson," said Basil. "Order, *Rodentia*. Family, *Zapodidae*. Genus, *Mus*. Species, *Neozapus*."

The Latin words made sense to me now, and I said, "J.J. took good care not to be seen walking, so no one could tell he was really—"

"—a North American jumping mouse!" said Basil. "By staying in that chair, he outwitted me, but next time we meet he'd better beware! Still, I should have deduced what he was."

"Nonsense! With twelve thousand mammals on earth, with species and sub-species ranging in size from a shrew to a whale, no one would fault you for not recognizing a jumping mouse."

We stared at the far-off figure, now just a small speck in the limitless sky.

"J.J. may stand for Jumpin' Joe," said Tom.

"Good guess," said someone. We turned, saw Peter Blau and ten mice, paws in the air.

"I rounded them up, Basil," said he. "Let's make a deal. Ask the law to go easy on me and I'll show where the smuggled stuff is stashed. J.J. hid it here and there, all over the ranch."

"Better tell it to the Sheriff, Blau. We're bringing you all in."

Moriarty mice cheered as we marched J.J.'s gang to the jailhouse. Shaw made a deal with Blau, to make sure that all the smuggled goods were returned to the Mexican museum, via CLOPS.

Back at camp Basil told Longfellow and Wenonah our jumping-mouse story. "Had I seen those long, strong legs earlier, my mission impossible might have been made possible. Next stop—Grand Canyon. Longfellow, you said back in Arizona that I had to choose Moriarty or the Canyon, because of your scheduled Texas trip. When's the next pony due here?"

"Not for a week. Take a shortcut through Texas."

"That's a long cut, not a shortcut," said I. "The Canyon's west of here—Texas lies east."

"True. But I'll pick up a cargo of cheese there, and deliver it to Hobbs, New Mexico. On my way to Hobbs I'll drop you off at Clovis. Trains are faster than our fastest ponies! Stow away on an Atchison, Topeka & Santa Fe train bound for Flagstaff, Arizona, near the Grand Canyon. You'll arrive in less than a week. Instead of waiting around for a pony, you'll be seeing Texas. What about it, Basil?"

"Done! We'll see your vast, sprawling Texas, which became a state on December 29, 1845. Ah, Texas! Stampedes, shootouts, square dances! Broncos, barbecues, bluebonnets!"

"Tall tales, tumbleweeds, tornadoes!" said I.

"Rangers, rustlers, roundups!" said Tom.

"Homesteads, heroes, he-men!" said Longfellow.

"He-mice, she-mice, free mice!" said Wenonah.

"Free to break camp and leave," said Basil.

We packed, doused the fire, and departed.

We left Wenonah and Tom at the mouse town of Palma, after we met their families and saw their school. The pony, too big to enter, waited outside.

"We're friends now, and we'll meet again," I told the couple, and Basil nodded agreement.

Then we mounted and rode into the night.

I dreamt of hungry jumping mice. I made them vanish by blinking twice. Had they been hungry jumping cats, I couldn't have made them vanish. In fact, I wouldn't be here to tell this tale.

STAMPEDE!

LONGFELLOW JOGGED, LOPED, TROTTED, GALLOPED, past Cuervo, Montoya, Tucamari, and then on to Glenrio, where we crossed over into Texas.

At dusk, under a deep purple sky, we reached our goal. Amarillo, mouse city, was like Amarillo, people city—bustling and lively.

The cheese was packed in saddlebags. Longfellow knelt, and warehouse mice, on ladders, slung the bags over his back, behind our howdah.

The next day found us riding along the prairie, miles and miles of it, with not a tree in sight.

Longfellow recited poems by his namesake, and Basil and I quoted our British poets. It was all so

42

harmonious that I couldn't help wishing the idyllic interlude would last forever.

Then the pony began reciting the poem *Excelsior,* written by the man Longfellow.

> The shades of night were falling fast
> As through an Alpine village passed
> A youth who bore, 'mid snow and ice,
> A banner with this strange device—
>> EXCELSIOR!

At that point, Basil's impish sense of humor prevailed, and he declaimed:

> The shades of day were swooping low
> As through a Texas town did go
> A mouse who bore, with other mice,
> No banner with a strange device,
> No ravioli, rolls, or rice,
> No soup, spaghetti, salt, or spice,
> But something extra-'specially nice,
> Beyond belief, above all price,
> Something straight from Paradise—
> A tasty, tempting ten-pound slice
>> OF GOUDA CHEESE!

43

"If it's Gouda 'nuff for thee, it's Gouda 'nuff for me!" I cried gleefully.

Longfellow's shoulders shook with mirth, so hard and so long that we slid off his back and rolled on the ground, helpless with laughter.

Our merriment ended with brutal suddenness!

Longfellow bent his head, put his ear to the ground, and listened.

"STAMPEDE!" he cried. "It's a mile away—I could hear the earth vibrating. We'll stay to one side 'til they pass, lest we be trampled."

We heard them before we saw them, for their thundering hooves shook the earth, sounded like a thousand lions roaring! Soon they appeared in the distance, row upon row of maddened beasts, surging forward, ever forward.

An anguished cry came from Longfellow.

"They're ponies, opera-loving ponies! I see my grandson Verdi right in the center of the front line with five of his friends—Rossini, Bellini, Puccini, Spontini, Cherubini! Operatic ponies are moody and temperamental. They are easily alarmed into stampeding. If Verdi falters, the panicky ponies behind may trample him. I must stop the stampede at once and save my grandson!"

Basil, who'd been staring at a hole in the ground, said, "I'll not let you risk your life! Wait here. Dawson and I will halt the stampede!"

"Mice stop a stampede? Impossible!"

His words fell on empty air. Basil had darted down the hole, in much the same way that Alice went down the rabbit hole.

I followed. In the half-darkness we raced along a maze of twisting, turning passageways. I was bewildered, but Basil seemed to know where he was headed. Was this a rabbit hole? Would we see Alice's famous Rabbit, and the equally famous Dormouse?

THE RESCUE
RIDERS

WE ENTERED A LARGE CHAMBER WHERE SUNLIGHT
filtered through a vent in the ceiling.

A grizzled old gopher faced us. His huge front
teeth made him look ferocious, but he spoke
kindly, in short, clipped sentences.

"Howdy! I'd know you two anywhere. Detective
Basil, Doc Dawson. I'm a professional digger. Dug
those fancy tunnels myself. Straight, slanty, up, down,
any which way. Reckon you aim to stop the stampede. Awful racket up there. I peeked. Ponies in
trouble. Longfellow's worried about Verdi, right?"

"Right. And I need help in a hurry."

"You bet. Feel the ground shake? Means the

ponies are near. Must find place for you to surface. Time's a-wastin'. My name's Augustus. To save time, call me Gus. C'mon!"

He burrowed along at fantastic speed. Dirt flew all around us, but not one speck touched us. His front teeth picked at the earth, his front claws shovelled it, his hind claws cast it behind him. At each vent he'd throw loose soil up to the surface to clear the tunnel.

The good-hearted gopher halted. "This is it, chums. On your own now. Best of luck!"

As Gus descended, we ascended, surfacing fifty yards to the left of the panting ponies.

They were pressed so closely together that their bodies formed a solid wall.

Racing toward them, we scurried up a pony's flank, then skipped ahead on other ponies' backs to reach Verdi, front row center.

"Dawson, stand at his left ear. I'll take his right. We're about to become opera stars. Pony Verdi loves opera written by Man Verdi. If music hath charms to soothe the savage breast, it should certainly soothe a stampeding pony."

"Basil, you're a genius! What a perfect rescue plan! Verdi's sure to respond, to slow his steps, little by little. The rest, opera-lovers all, will do the same. Shall we begin with the aria *La Donna Mobile,* from the opera *Rigoletto?* Downbeat, Maestro, please!"

So commenced one of my strangest experiences, one I shall never forget.

Singing one's heart out while clinging to a galloping pony's ear is far from easy. It's downright dangerous, especially when one reaches for high notes. (I happen to be a tenor.) We rocked and rolled like sailors in a stormy sea!

But the Rescue Riders, Brave Basil and Daring Dawson, sang gallantly on! Magical melodies from *Aida, La Traviata, Il Trovatore,* and other operas composed by Verdi. The musician, then in his eighties, lived in Milan, Italy. Had he heard us singing his works that day, he would have been proud.

Our reward came when someone began singing along with us. It was the pony Verdi, singing softly so as not to drown us out. We patted his mane to encourage him. Soon his friends Rossini and Bellini joined in, then Puccini and Spontini and Cherubini, and then all the rest of the ponies.

The more they sang, the more slowly they moved, going from a gallop to a canter to a trot to a jog to a standstill.

The stampede was over!

10

THE HAUNTED
HOTEL MYSTERY

AFTER THE FOND REUNION OF GRANDFATHER AND grandson, we were praised to the skies.

"I just used my horse sense," declared the detective modestly.

The ponies asked him to play his flute.

"My name's Humperdinck," said one. "Please play the *Children's Prayer,* from the opera *Hansel and Gretel.* My namesake, Engelbert Humperdinck, wrote it two years ago, in 1893."

Basil nodded. "A charming opera! I'll play after Dawson fetches Gus the Gopher. Without his help, you might still be stampeding, half-dead from exhaustion, or badly hurt."

He played after Gus arrived. Rabbits and prairie dogs and other gophers came out of their holes to hear the lovely, lilting music.

Everyone begged him to play on, but he said he was late for a date at a haunted hotel.

Longfellow dropped us off at Clovis, New Mexico. Parting was sad, but we promised to keep in touch through CLOPS, and meet again.

We stole aboard an Atchison, Topeka & Santa Fe train going west, and perched on a windowsill near some empty seats.

Basil said, "The stampede's not really a case, because no criminals were involved."

"On the contrary! Fear and panic were the criminals, robbing ponies of the power to think clearly. You did what Sherlock Holmes would do. You observed the stampede, analyzed its elements, and deduced the way to halt it."

"You're right, but my mind's elsewhere, at the hotel. I should have been there long ago."

"But you've been busy tracking down smugglers, jailing a few, breaking up the ring, and stopping a stampede. My dear detective, you haven't been exactly idle!"

"True, and it was exciting and challenging. But there's a law of averages. The next case will no doubt be boring, dull as dishwater, about as simple as learning one's ABC's."

He was wrong! Difficult, dangerous, dramatic, the case demanded all his sleuthing skill.

Tired, I slept. I have two favorite dreams. In one, in a London factory, I hold the same high position Basil's cousin Anatole has in a Paris factory—First Vice-President in Charge of Cheese-Tasting. In the second, I am at a royal banquet, judging cheeses of all nations.

On the train I had the second dream. Wearing a judge's badge, I was sampling peppery Pepato from Italy when a voice broke into my dream.

"Hello up there! May we sit with you?"

A handsome American military mouse stood below, with his wife and young daughter.

Basil beckoned, and the trio joined us.

"I'm Jim Gillen. It's an honor to meet Basil of Baker Street, and his associate, Dr. Dawson."

"The honor is ours, Colonel, judging by the many medals on your uniform," replied Basil.

The child held out a notebook and a pencil.

"Please, sir? My friends won't believe I've met you unless I show them your autograph."

Smiling, the sleuth signed his name with a flourish. Then, at Gillen's request, we both signed his copy of *Basil and the Cave of Cats*.

They were bound for Fort Tillamook, Oregon.

Told of our destination, Gillen looked grim.

"We were at the Hathaway Hotel ten days ago. Planned to stay two weeks, but left in two days. Couldn't stomach what went on there."

"Tell me about it, Colonel," said Basil.

At mention of the Hathaway, his daughter's eyes widened in terror. Bursting into sobs, she buried her head in her mother's lap.

"Fran, do comfort Alexandra," said Gillen to his wife. "We'll go below, out of earshot."

Standing in the aisle of the swaying train, we listened to Gillen's strange story.

"My child is terrified, and even I, a down-to-earth soldier, shuddered when I saw the beast that haunts the Hathaway.

"We called it the *Thing*. It stalks by night on a clifftop opposite the hotel. It's monstrously tall, with glaring eyes and blood-red lips. A greenish glow always surrounds it. Some mice thought it a ghost or a demon, others said it was an alien from outer space. Which? I don't honestly know. The weird noises it made! Wild, crazy laughter that sent chills chasing up one's spine, mournful howls and yowls, bloodcurdling shrieks.

"The Thorbridges opened the hotel a year ago. It was an instant success. We've stayed there twice, and enjoyed it. But then the *Thing* came, two months ago. Business is so bad now that the hotel may close its doors forever."

Basil said, "It was once Lord Hathaway's villa. When he became Ambassador to Mexico, he moved away, leaving a caretaker. His lordship wasn't told that the caretaker died. Outlaws made the villa a hideout, let it go to rack and ruin. He finally found out. The Thorbridges, his cook and butler, longed to run a hotel. He sold them the villa for one dollar, provided they restore it to its former beauty."

Gillen nodded. "And they did, spent their life savings on plumbers, painters, carpenters, gardeners. They put in new doors, floors, windows, tiled the walls, bought costly furnishings. Now, alas, because of the *Thing*—"

"FLAGSTAFF!" called the conductor.

We grabbed our bags and left the train. Local mice led us to a CLOPS pony called Keats. It was eighty miles out to the Grand Canyon.

At the hotel, all was chaos and confusion.

56

Crowds of grumpy guests clutching their bags paced the front veranda, waiting for a pony to carry them away.

Off to one side stood two dignified mice, unmistakably British. She, in a long black bombazine dress with lace trim, stayed serene amid all the turmoil. He, in tweeds, surveyed the departing mice calmly through his monocle.

Basil doffed his deerstalker cap and bowed.

"Mr. and Mrs. Thorbridge, I presume?"

11

THE THING ON
THE CLIFF

THORBRIDGE BEAMED, AND HELD OUT HIS PAW.

"Welcome! His lordship wrote of your coming. You should know that there are those who say the *Thing* is supernatural. Poppycock! Sir, I'm firmly convinced it was made by mice!"

Basil nodded. "Precisely my own opinion."

"It's teatime," said our host. "Shall I have the tea cart wheeled into the rose garden?"

Soon we were sipping real English tea as our awed eyes beheld the mighty Grand Canyon.

Fabulous? Fantastic? Majestic? Magnificent? All of these! Fifty-six miles long, a mile deep, covering a thousand square miles, its vast, spectacular sweep is beyond belief.

Nature had sculpted cliffs, chasms, buttes, ledges, mountains. Wildflowers abounded, in riots of color, and cactus plants as tall as trees. Dazzled, I decided no place on earth was more beautiful than the Grand Canyon.

The hotel was on a clifftop, opposite another cliff, wild and craggy, with no pathways. Basil looked across the deep gorge separating the two.

"Is that where the *Thing* appears, Thorbridge?"

"Yes. Before it came we housed two hundred guests. Now there are only nine."

"By tonight I'd like a list of their names, and facts about them. How large is your staff?"

"Seven stayed on, old friends we worked with in England, who are quite above suspicion."

"Then no staff list is needed. Tonight Dawson and I will observe the *Thing*. I'll use a powerful spyglass to confirm my theories."

At midnight, hidden behind some bushes, we gazed at the cliff opposite. We had not long to wait. Out of the sinister shadows came the *Thing*, like the personification of all evil.

A monstrous head crowned a tall, grotesquely thin body that stalked stiffly along, surrounded by a sickly greenish glow. Eyes rolling, lips set in a loathsome grin, it befouled the night air with hideous howls and eerie shrieks. Basil said it was not supernatural, but was he wrong?

What was it? I knew not, but it was the stuff of

which nightmares are made. Chills chased up and down my spine. I jumped when Basil touched me.

"Let the *Thing* think we're terrified," whispered he. "Shiver and shake as you make a mad dash for the hotel. Can you act the part?"

I broke all speed records sprinting toward the hotel, and my shivers and shakes were not an act.

We pushed the heavy hotel doors open.

Behind the marble reception desk stood our hosts. Candlelight revealed brocaded sofas, carved oaken tables, walls of Italian tile, statues, and paintings.

"The *Thing* is cleverly constructed," Basil said. "An ingenious mechanism rolls the eyes. Luminous paint produces that greenish glow."

"Copycats, or copymice!" I cried. "The idea for the glow comes from a Sherlock Holmes case, *Hound of the Baskervilles*. The villain there used something similar—phosphorous paste."

Basil asked about the two guards, Pat Martin and Mike Mullen. Thorbridge said they were on duty day and night because of the hotel safe.

"The criminals crave a bigger prize than the valuables in your hotel safe," said Basil. "This was once a deserted villa. Who stayed here, and when? What's hidden here, and where? I'll find clues to the past tomorrow, by studying old newspaper files."

The wall behind the desk held shelves divided into compartments for keys and mail. Thorbridge reached in to remove a typewritten sheet.

"Sir, here is the list you requested."

The sleuth scanned it. "Hmm. Interesting, but I'm half asleep. Good night, one and all!"

12

TOO MANY
SUSPECTS

SMILING HAPPILY, MRS. THORBRIDGE SERVED US breakfast in our rooms the next day.

"Sir, you've given us hope," she told Basil.

"I echo Ivy's words," declared her husband. "And sir, my friends call me Thor."

"Friends Thor and Ivy, skip the 'sir.' Call me Basil. This morning I'll hunt for clues to the past, at the morgue."

Ivy arched her eyebrows. "The *morgue?*"

"It's not as ghoulish as it sounds," replied the detective. "A morgue is a newspaper's library, where back issues are filed away. Nothing's deader than yesterday's news, so it's called the morgue. But before I leave, let's look over the list, and my notes."

GUEST LIST

ALFRED AND LYNN GILMORE

Famous retired actors. They give play readings for our guests, so pay lower rates. Have stayed a year, since hotel opened.

COMMENT: Retired actors may need money. Did criminals hire them to do the Thing's *voices, she the screams, he the groans?*

COUNTESS DE LA POULIGNY-ST. PIERRE

Of Touraine, France. Wants to buy hotel, convert it to villa, live in it. Offered huge sum. We refused. Here six months.

COMMENT: Resents Thorbridges, anxious to acquire hotel for her American home. Wealthy, able to hire criminals to haunt hotel.

DONALD RICKSON

Handsome young American artist. Sells a painting now and then. Loves the Grand Canyon, keeps painting it. Here three months.

COMMENT: The Thing's *ghastly face and greenish glow have made many mice leave. An artist could easily produce these weird effects. Does he need extra money? Have the criminals hired him?*

DEBORAH AND AUGUST BERGER

Hotel owners. Dallas-Stilton, Denver-Stilton, Pasadena-Stilton. Keep offering low price for our hotel. Here a year, off and on.

COMMENT: Is the Thing *their idea? If hotel closes, they'd buy it cheaply, change name to Grand Canyon-Stilton for their chain.*

MARY ANN GOODE

Pretty young Boston librarian, here for her health. Canyon climate beneficial. Terrified of the *Thing,* but too shy to adjust to strangers at another hotel, so stays. Here three months.

COMMENT: Her health's improving, but if so terrified, why not change hotels? Possibility——is she in love with young Rickson?

FATIMA DOMIATI AND OSMAN DURAK

She works at Egyptian Embassy in Washington, he at Turkish Embassy. Met here, claim love at first sight. Here two months.

COMMENT: Foreign agents? Canyon of military value? Unlikely.

Basil discussed his notes with Thor. Then they conferred in low tones until I heard the sleuth say, "The pantry? Agreed. Cheerio!"

He waved goodbye and was off like a shot.

On the veranda Don Rickson and I had a talk ranging from Cheshire cheese to Cheshire cats. He was so sincere and so charming that I felt like crossing his name off the suspect list.

The Countess joined us. Dark eyes dancing, she related amusing experiences she'd had in Santa Barbara. She, too, was a charmer.

Still, one didn't eliminate suspects because of their winning ways. I'd met charming criminals who were unbelievably evil. From now on I'd leave such judgments to the expert, Basil.

We went walking, and met veiled Fatima and turbaned Osman, who said he'd known Basil abroad.

The luncheon gong sounded as we neared the hotel. The others entered, but I waited for Basil. After twenty minutes I went inside, and was still nibbling away at my first course when the Countess and Rickson waved on their way out.

At last Basil came, apologizing, just as Fatima and Osman approached our table.

"Basil, I'm Osman Durak. In the Case of the Persian Tentmaker, in 1892, a Turkish policemouse was your interpreter. Do you remember me?"

"Your face, but not your name. Good to see you! I've since mastered the Turkish tongue."

"I knew you would, Basil. May I present my fiancée, Fatima Domiati? She was the first female policemouse in all Egypt."

Fatima smiled. "I am honored! Will you unravel this mystery in record time?"

"Alas, no. Too many tangled threads, too many loose ends. However, you've made my task easier. Ex-policemice don't belong on my suspect list. I'll remove both your names at once."

Osman bowed. "A thousand thanks! I'd offer to assist you, but we leave for Washington today, to be married at the Egyptian Embassy."

After they'd gone up to pack, Basil remarked, "I ran into the Countess. Small world! Years ago I knew her in Paris under her stage name, Renée Vernet, when she was a ballerina. Lost track of her for ages. Now she's the widow of a count, and a good friend of my sister Bryna. She's off the list. Also cross off—"

"Young Don Rickson?" I asked eagerly.

"Good thinking! When I searched his room—"

I was surprised. "You searched his room?"

"All the rooms but one. Not a job I fancy, but I had to do it, because clues were too few. I returned when the gong sounded, used the kitchen entrance. Thor met me in the pantry, as planned. I nosed about while everyone was at lunch. Rickson's in the clear. A letter from his art professor praised his fine character, and other letters offered high prices for his paintings. He's well-off, doesn't have to earn extra money working for criminals. And in his college yearbook, his class-mates nicknamed him 'Honest Don.' Fellow students usually zero in on a mouse's true self."

Consulting my list, I crossed out Fatima, Osman, the Countess, and young Rickson.

"Five names remain, Basil. Lynn and Alfred Gilmore, Deborah and August Berger, and Miss Goode. Which one's your chief suspect?"

He grinned. "My dear doctor, that's for me to know and for you to find out."

"At least tell me this—male or female?"

"You'll know in due time, Dawson."

My temper flared. "As usual, it pleases you to keep me in suspense. I work side by side with you, obey your every command, even run your errands. Yet I'm left dangling in the dark, without a clue! You take devilish delight in never telling me who's guilty 'til the mystery's practically solved! Unfair, Sir Know-It-All, unfair! As the mice of Ireland say—*the back of me paw to ye!*"

My friend leaned forward, eyes agleam.

"Ah, but my way is so much more exciting and dramatic for you! You yearn to know the answer, you burn with curiosity as to who the culprit can be. A suspect smiles, and you wonder what it signifies. You read signs of guilt in the smallest act—a raised eyebrow, a sidelong glance, a trembling of lips. Your senses are sharpened, your mind's alerted and aroused! Come now, isn't it far more interesting than knowing the ending ahead of time?"

I tried again. "All hail, Sherlock Holmes of the Mouse World! Won't you reward your faithful Dr. Dawson with a wee little clue?"

"I will not! Sherlock Holmes keeps his faithful Dr. Watson in suspense. What's fit for Watson should be fit for Dawson!"

"Then finish your cheesecake and let's go," said I, crossly. "We're the last ones in the dining room."

Outside, the Countess and Rickson said they were leaving that afternoon. The day's mail had brought news of a seaside villa for sale in Santa Barbara, and an invitation for Rickson to hold a one-mouse show of his Canyon paintings at a museum. We wished them luck, and went out on the veranda. Over to one side sat the five suspects, rocking away.

Basil whispered, "I'll join the rocking-chair brigade. Any information I pick up will help in the final solution. And you?"

I yawned, sank into a chair. "I'll catnap over here while you mouse around over there."

He left me. Voices came faintly from the other end of the veranda. A game was being played. One of the group would quote a line from a play by Shakespeare, and then ask another mouse to name the play and also the act in which the line was spoken. Interested, I tried to stay awake.

"*To be or not to be.* Miss Goode?"

"From HAMLET, Act III. It's my turn to quote. *Not a mouse stirring.* Mr. Gilmore?"

"Also from HAMLET. Act I, Scene I. *Parting is such sweet sorrow.* For you, Mrs. Berger."

"ROMEO AND JULIET. Act I, Scene II. Here's a long one. *Double, double toil and trouble; Fire burn and cauldron bubble.* Mrs. Gilmore?"

70

"MACBETH. Act IV, Scene I. *Villainy, Villainy, Villainy!* For Basil of Baker Street."

"OTHELLO. Act V, Scene II. *See, how she leans her cheek upon her hand.* Miss Goode?"

"From—oh, yes—ROMEO AND JULIET. Act II. *Come on, and kiss me, Kate.* Mr. Berger."

"TAMING OF THE SHREW. Act V, Scene II. *Good Titus, dry thine eyes.* Basil, please."

"Elementary, my dear Berger. It's from TITUS ANDRONICUS. Act III, Scene I. *The long days task is done and we must sleep—*"

Ah, sleep! The words had a hypnotic effect. My head fell forward on my chest, and I slept, I know not for how long.

A gentle tapping on my shoulder awoke me.

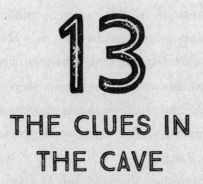

THE CLUES IN
THE CAVE

I OPENED MY EYES. BASIL STOOD AT MY SIDE, TAPPING
me with a coil of rope.

"The others are resting in their rooms," he
said, "but you and I will hike to the crossroads and
descend into a deep gorge."

I arose. "In the words of the great bard Shakespeare, *Lead on, Macduff!* From *Macbeth*. Never
mind which act or which scene. Let's go!"

On the way Basil revealed what he'd learned
at the morgue. Two years ago Monterey Jack, a
mouse outlaw from Monterey, California, had fled
to Arizona. He and his gang then used Hathaway's
abandoned villa as their hideout.

Handsome but tricky, Jack would go to a town alone, posing as a rich, retired miner eager to marry. He'd court females who worked in banks and jewelry stores. Questioning them cleverly, he'd learn when cash or gem shipments were due. Then he'd vanish, returning with his gang to rob. After scores of holdups, they were jailed. As for the loot, the outlaws refused to tell where it was hidden. Law-mice searched the villa, but in vain.

Basil unfolded a plan of the hotel's main floor, pointed to the enormous reception hall.

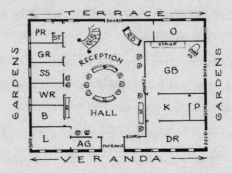

LEGEND:	MAIN FLOOR	HATHAWAY HOTEL
DR DINING ROOM	L LIBRARY	P PANTRY
GB GRAND BALLROOM	AG ART GALLERY	O OFFICE
GS GRAND STAIRCASE	B BOOKSHOP	ST STORAGE
RD RECEPTION DESK	WR WRITING ROOM	S SOFA
K KITCHEN	SS SOUVENIR SHOP	C CHAIR
PR POWDER ROOM	GR GAME ROOM	

"Mark my words! When the villa was remodeled, the hiding place of the loot was somehow covered up. I learned that Jack and two of his gang escaped *three* months ago. The hauntings began *two* months ago. Clearly, Jack arranged the hauntings in order to get at his loot!

"Dawson, I deduce that the money and the jewels are in the one place guarded day and night—the reception hall! And Monterey Jack himself will lead us to the hiding place! Not willingly, of course—I'll have to trick him.

"But look, we're at the gorge separating the two cliffs. Observe the cliff on which the hotel stands. It slopes, so one can ascend or descend. The other is straight up and down, practically perpendicular. Thor says no mouse has ever climbed it. Three mice fell to their deaths trying. Too perilous, by far!"

I nodded. "Yet the *Thing* gets up there, time after time. Might there be a narrow opening in the base of that cliff, barely wide enough for a mouse's body to squeeze through?"

"We'll investigate," said Basil, uncoiling the rope. He tied one end around a tree trunk, then peered into the depths of the gorge, and let the rest of the rope drop.

We went down, paw over paw. It was a long haul, but at last we stood on solid ground.

Circling the base of the cliff, we tugged at the dense underbrush that covered it, pulling at boughs and twigs and leaves. It was tiring, tedious work, but we kept at it.

Then Basil cried, "Eureka! An opening near the ground! Lie flat and squirm through."

We emerged in a high-ceilinged cave. Food and clothes were strewn about. Some light came from a tunnel leading to another cave, which we entered. Part of the second cave had no ceiling. We peered upward and saw the source of the light—a long, slender shaft that reached to the clifftop. Craning our necks, we spied a patch of blue sky far above.

Basil said, "The shaft was created eons ago. An earthquake probably made a small crack in the clifftop. Rocks and earth tumbled down, collapsing part of this cave's ceiling. Some Canyon Indians were cave dwellers. To let in the light, they removed the rocks and the dirt. Wind and rain gradually widened the shaft."

We looked upward again. The shaft was like a long tunnel standing on end. And now we noticed a series of small platforms and trapezes, fastened to the walls of the shaft!

"Only circus mice would dare use trapezes so high up," said I. "Did the newspapers mention any ex-trapeze artists in Jack's gang?"

"Yes, Gideon and Gabriel Gribble, nicknamed Giddy and Gabby. They did other acts, too. Giddy was a stiltwalker, Gabby a ventriloquist. Stilts explain the *Thing's* height, and a ventriloquist could easily do the voices."

"Then stilts and costume must be on top of the cliff," said I, "waiting for the daring young mice on the flying trapeze to swing through the air with the greatest of ease—"

"Ssh, someone's out there," whispered Basil. "We're trapped—it's our only exit. Listen."

"Gabby, I'm so fed up with doing the *Thing*. When can we quit and go after the loot?"

"Sis says soon, Giddy. Hey, here's Jack. Boss, when can we quit hauntin' the hotel?"

77

"Real soon. Can't wait to get my paws on those sparklers. The cash is long gone, but we've got a fortune in diamonds and stuff."

"Swell, Jack. Say, I sure am sleepy. Giddy and I never get enough shut-eye lately."

"Same here, guys. Let's all take a snooze."

"What fantastic luck!" said Basil in my ear. "We'd be in deadly danger if they captured us!"

We waited, then tiptoed into the outer cave. Flat on their backs lay the three sleeping beauties, snoring in three different keys.

Basil bowed low and whispered, "Sleep well, sweet scoundrels! We'll meet again!"

14

A TRAP FOR
MONTEREY JACK

BACK AT THE HOTEL, BASIL TOLD THE THORBRIDGES
the next step of his strategy.

"Thor, announce at dinner tonight that because
of the *Thing* you are out of business. Tell them that
tomorrow afternoon the Hathaway Hotel closes
its doors forever, that at four Keats of CLOPS will
transport guests, staff, and luggage to Flagstaff. Also
mention that later a pony named Yeats will come for
the two guards, the four of us, and Miss Goode."

"Why is Miss Goode staying?" I asked.

"Frankly, Miss Goode's no good. I'll say no
more now, but shall confront her tomorrow."

After Thor's announcement, most mice went

up to pack. At midnight the *Thing* began to stalk to and fro on the craggy cliff opposite.

"This is its last show, to make sure everyone leaves," said Basil as we watched from our window. "The outlaws' informant has told them the hotel closes tomorrow. They'll come after the loot tomorrow night. Little do they dream that we'll be here to welcome them!"

We played chess the next afternoon. At three Basil consulted the gold watch given him by a mouse duke whose kidnapped son he'd rescued.

"Hmm. Time to visit Miss Mary Ann Goode. Come along, Dawson—the game is afoot. Or should I say—the *dame* is afoot?"

"Only if she's standing," said I, with a smirk.

As planned, the Thorbridges joined us.

Miss Goode was cordial. "Do sit down. I'm glad lonely little me will travel with you. Ivy and Thor, how sad that you must close your hotel! I've loved it here, and my health has improved. Can you suggest another nice hotel?"

"Try the Graybar Hotel," said the detective, in tones as cold as ice.

"The Graybar? Thanks. Where is it, please?"

"There are many, Miss Goode. Hotel Graybar is what criminals say when they mean prison."

"But what would *I* know about prison?"

"As much as Giddy and Gabby know——*Sis!*"

"Giddy? Gabby? Sis? I don't understand."

"Bunk! The false bottom of your trunk had newspaper stories about the fake diamonds used in your circus act, The Flying Gribbles. Monterey Jack had a sweetheart—you! Picking up the loot would get you real diamonds, but first you had to get rid of the Thorbridges."

She sank down on the bed, sobbing softly.

"What dreadful lies! I'm Mary Ann Goode, a Boston librarian, here to recover my health."

"To recover your wealth! You're no librarian! You masterminded the prison break, the *Thing,* the stilts, the luminous paint! You're the brains behind the whole plot. Don't deny it, Mary Ann Goode, alias Gertie Gribble, alias Gaudy Gertie!"

She whipped off her glasses, reached under the pillow. A pearl-handled pistol appeared in her paw, pointed straight at Basil.

"You snoopy Sherlock! Paws up, all of you! I love Jack and I love diamonds! Tonight we get the loot, includin' the diamonds Jack said I'll wear at our weddin'! Not even Queen Victoria can stop us, you bloomin' Britishers!"

I groaned. Was this snarling spitfire to triumph? And then I heard the horrible sounds, the most terrifying on earth to mice.

"MEOW! M E O W!! MEEEEEEEEEEEEE-OWWWWWWWW!!!"

Startled, Gertie dropped her gun.

The meowing stopped as Ivy picked it up and said sweetly, "Gertie darlin', that was a bloomin' British cat! I did the meowing myself."

"Good work, Ivy," said Basil. "Tie Mary Ann Bad to a chair. She'll have a front-row seat tonight when her partners walk into our trap."

Keats came at four and was soon on his way, laden down with mice and their belongings.

That night we lit no lights. The guards, Pat Martin and Mike Mullen, and the rest of us hid behind sofas in the reception hall. Gaudy Gertie sat in a chair, bound and gagged.

At last the outlaws swaggered in, with a lantern. We peeked, saw Jack go behind the reception desk and yank hard at the shelves that held keys and mail. The wood splintered as he wrenched the shelves off the tiled wall.

Out came his knife, to pry away at six tiles until they loosened. He removed them, and we saw bricks behind. Again he pried away, this time at the bricks, until he was able to lift them off.

And there was the secret hiding place! The bricks he'd removed weren't solid. They were only fronts that concealed a hollow space!

He reached into that space for a long tin box, which he opened. His paws dipped into it, clutched greedily at necklaces, bracelets, rings, tiaras, at diamonds and emeralds and rubies, all glittering and gleaming by lantern light!

Giddy spoke. "Divvy it up, Jack! Half fer me

and Gabby, half fer you and Sis. You promised! C'mon, divvy up the sparklers!"

But Jack picked up the box and drew a gun.

"Sorry, pals. It's for me and my Mexican honey!"

"You dirty double-crosser!" yelled Giddy.

"You lyin' lowdown cheat!" screamed Gabby.

Jack laughed. "Your lives aren't worth a plugged nickel. One move and you're dead!"

It was then that Basil leaped out, waving a rifle, which he jabbed into Jack's back.

"One move, and *you're* dead! Drop the box and the gun, and put your paws up! Reach!"

The box and the gun landed on the floor, but the wily bandit tricked Basil by kicking over the lantern. In the darkness I heard scuffling sounds, and the slam of a door.

At last Thor lit a candle. The guards had caught Giddy and Gabby, but their chief had escaped!

Basil looked glum. "The loot's here, but not the head looter. J.J. escaped me, too. If those two scalawags ever meet and team up, there'll be trouble, and plenty of it!"

(He predicted rightly. Jack and J.J. did meet, and joined with Ratigan to form the Anti-Basil League, but that's another story.)

Once ungagged, Gertie glared at us, and gave us her opinion of Monterey Jack.

"That two-faced two-timer, ditchin' me for another dame! Why, he's lower than a snake's belly! That slimy skunk, that lyin' lizard! That ornery rat has ruined my life!"

"You ruined it yourself by becoming a criminal," Basil said sternly. "You can think about it in your new home, the Hotel Graybar."

The words of her reply were so foul that I decline to soil this page with them.

15

CALIFORNIA
CALLING!

AT BREAKFAST THE NEXT MORNING BASIL TOLD US
how Shakespeare had helped him solve the case.

"Gertie came upstairs early when I searched
the rooms, so I had to skip hers. Later, on the
veranda, I was introduced to the shy, soft-spoken
mouse who seemed to fear her own shadow. She
had me fooled until we began the Shakespeare
game.

"I soon saw that the Gilmores, the Bergers, and
myself knew the plays as well as we knew cheese.
Goode did not. We quoted word for word. She did
not. We made no mistakes. She did, naming the
wrong play once and the wrong act twice. Also,

although it wasn't necessary, we always mentioned from which scene of an act Shakespeare's line came. Goode never did this.

"Strange, thought I. *A librarian would know her Shakespeare, would she not?* I talked of the *Thing*. She had hysterics. Was it an act? Had her hysterics in the past made mice leave?

"I had to search her room! Luckily, she took a stroll after the game. You were still asleep. In her trunk were write-ups and photos. Our shy, soft-spoken librarian was the high-flying Gaudy Gertie, sister of Giddy and Gabby, and Jack's sweetheart. All became clear as crystal! To close the case, I had to track down the *Thing*. I woke you, Dawson, and—to quote the title of one of Shakespeare's plays—ALL'S WELL THAT ENDS WELL."

"Basil," said Ivy, "you've made our lives happy again. Name your fee."

"My fee is a favor. Too many mice and men say 'Holmes,' without the 'Mr.' Lamentable lack of respect! The favor? Give your place a new name—the Mr. Holmes Hotel."

"Done!" cried Thor. "We'll also have the Basil Ballroom and the Dawson Dining Hall. Think of

the Mr. Holmes Hotel as your second home—
you'll always be welcome here!"

And so we sampled life in Arizona for a few
weeks. We rafted on the Colorado River rapids,
hiked up and down the Canyon, read the Canyon's
history. Basil kept doling out stray facts.

"Do you know the Canyon's age? It's only seven
million years old! Know the Hassayampa River
legend? Those who drink its waters can never
tell the truth again! Want to know how Flagstaff
was named? On July 4, 1876, some Arizonans
trimmed a tall pine and shaped it into a staff. They
flew a flag from it to celebrate. Others settled
near the pine. The town that sprang up was called
Flagstaff."

"All play and no work makes a dull mouse,"
said Basil one day, as we sipped tea in the garden.
"Ivy and Thor, you're perfect hosts, but we must
travel on. I'm seldom content unless I have a case
to challenge me, a knotty problem to solve. So
we'll be moving on, but where? By Jove, Dawson,
my question's answered! Look down the path—
Longfellow's heading this way! And unless I miss

my guess, he brings news of someone in need of
my sleuthing skill."

Basil was right. Mice on Catalina Island, off
California's coast, had seen lights out at sea, blinking this message in Morse code:

BASIL I NEED YOUR HELP PLEASE COME JEANNIE

"A damsel in distress, a friend in trouble,"
declared Basil. "We'll go to her aid at once."

"Is Jeannie a Scottish mouse?" asked Thor.

"Scottish, but no mouse. Two-headed Jeannie
is the niece of the Loch Ness Monster."

"Fancy that!" said Ivy. "Well, it's plain to see

that there's never a dull moment in *your* life, Basil of Baker Street!"

Within the hour we were on Longfellow's back, hitting the trail at a gallop.

"California, here we come!" I cried.

Ahead lay another adventure.

Read more about Basil,
the mouse detective, in . . .

Basil and the Lost Colony

AMBUSHED!

AN ARROW WITH STRANGE MARKINGS WAS THE CLUE that sent Basil of Baker Street scurrying off to Switzerland in search of the Lost Colony.

Some mice claim that the Sealed Mousehole Mystery best displayed Basil's genius. I beg to differ. The Case of the Lost Colony was clearly the most extraordinary exploit of this extraordinary detective.

Did it not take him to another land, to lead an expedition of thirty-two mice up a towering mountain? Was he not pursued by Professor Ratigan, sinister ruler of the mouse underworld?

And what of the shaggy mouse? Were it not

for Basil, the giant creature might never have—

But I fear I am scampering ahead of my tale. . . .

It all began in London, England, on a chill April afternoon in the year 1891.

I, Dr. David Q. Dawson, sat alone before the fire. The cozy flat Basil and I shared was in the model mouse town of Holmestead, erected on a high shelf in the cellar of Baker Street, Number 221B.

Abovestairs lived Basil's hero, Mr. Sherlock Holmes. There my friend learned all his detective lore by listening as the great man discussed his cases with his associate, Dr. Watson. It was not surprising, therefore, that Basil came to be called the Sherlock Holmes of the Mouse World.

This afternoon he prowled the streets of London, tracking Professor Ratigan's gang. He had jailed all but the Professor and two gangsters. Suddenly I heard unsteady steps on the stair—could it be Basil? I flung the door wide—it was he!

Face scratched, clothes torn, he staggered inside.

"Ambushed! Ambushed by a starving Siamese!"

His whiskers twitched. "I turned a corner on Stilton Square, and two blue eyes met mine. A voice said, 'Basil of Baker Street, I presume?' I nodded.

"'I've been expecting you,' said the Siamese softly.

"Then it sprang, but I sprang faster, down through a crack in the pavement. Back and forth above me moved the kitten's claw. 'This cat-and-mouse game is not for you,' I told myself. I raced along underground and climbed up on James Street.

"But the Siamese spied me! My dear doctor, have you ever seen a kitten coming toward you at a full gallop? It's a sight I would sooner forget!"

He sighed, and sank back in his chair.

"End the suspense, Basil—how did you escape?"

He winked. "I didn't. The cat ate me."

"Stop joking, Basil. What did you do?"

"Dawson, I am always prepared for emergencies. In my pocket was a packet of catnip. I tore it open, tossed it at the monster, and fled. Clearly, the cat preferred catnip to mousenip, else I should not be here to tell the tale."

His eyes narrowed to slits. "That ambush was arranged! In all England, there is only one mouse who can bargain safely with cats, only one mouse who owns a suit of armor—the villainous Professor Ratigan!"

"Armor stolen from the British Mousmopolitan Museum," said I. "It's a pity that this brilliant Ratcliffe graduate chose a life of crime. You've been trailing him and his gang for weeks, and you're exhausted. Let the police finish the job. The International Society of Mouse Mountaineers meets in Switzerland next week. Climbing an alp or two will make a new mouse of you!"

"No doubt, Dawson, but the old one will have to do. I'll not leave London until Ratigan is behind bars. Meanwhile, I shall seek relaxation. Mr. Holmes relaxes with indoor pistol practice, but I prefer the bow and arrow."

The target was an oil painting of a horned owl. A crack shot, Basil was also a walking encyclopedia on the history of archery.

PING! An arrow whizzed past my right ear. PING! Another shot past my left. PING! PING!

The arrows flashed by, faster and faster. I began to feel as though *I* might turn out to be the target, instead of the owl. I feared to remain in my chair, and I feared to rise from it.

"Really, Basil! Why don't you practice outdoors,

as William Tell did? Spare me! Next you'll place a grape upon my helpless head, and aim at it!"

"Splendid idea, Dawson, but it must wait."

He had put down his bow, and was peering intently out of the front window.

"A client approaches," he said. "Seems like a likely looking fellow. However, unless the case concerns the Professor, I shall decline it. Nothing must halt me in my pursuit of the ruthless Ratigan!"

THE MYSTERIOUS
ARROW

THE BELL CLANGED. SOON MRS. JUDSON, OUR mousekeeper, rapped on the door and admitted a caller.

Basil rose to shake paws with a tall, muscular mouse.

"Good day," said the stranger. "You are Basil?"

"I am, sir. Your studies at the British Mousmopolitan must be fascinating. But do you not long for the colder climes of your native Norway?"

"I do indeed. We've never met—how did you know?"

Basil smiled. "It's unseasonably cold for April. The mice outside wear coats. You do not, yet your paws are warm. Your slight accent is Norwegian, and the envelope you hold bears the Mousmopolitan imprint."

The caller beamed. "What more did you deduce?"

"That you are Edvard Hagerup, from Tromsö, near the Arctic, an author who writes about the cat family. Your hobby is our national game of cricket."

"Amazing! Astounding! Astonishing!" cried Hagerup.

"Elementary, my dear author. I observed, I analyzed, I deduced. Dangling from your watch chain is the Award of the Golden Cheddar. In 1888 Edvard Hagerup of Tromsö won it for his fine book, *Our Feline Foes*. I perceive a pamphlet in your pocket, entitled *The Sticky Wicket in Cricket*. This tells me your hobby."

"Remarkable, Basil! And your own hobby is archery. That is why the Museum sent me to see you."

He took a sheet of paper from the envelope he held.

"Be good enough to read this aloud, Basil." The detective did so:

Dear Mice of the Mousmopolitan--

My sister and I are retired English
schoolmistresses, now living in
Switzerland. The subjects we taught
were botany and zoology.

We enjoy mountain climbing. One day,
rounding a rock, we came face to face
with a giant shaggy mouse. He had a
shovel-shaped tail, long white fur,
and stood <u>seven</u> inches high!

In his arms was a little lost mouse!
Thrusting the child at us, he fled,
vanishing from sight above the
snowline. The villagers say he often
returns lost mouselings, fleeing
before he can be thanked. He is of no
known species, and they named him
the Adorable Snowmouse.

In his haste he dropped an arrow,
which we enclose. Its design is
unlike any we have ever seen. Also
enclosed is a sketch of the Snowmouse,
which we did from memory.

What do you scientists make of all this?

Yours most anxiously,

Flora and Fauna Faversham

Basil rubbed his chin thoughtfully. "Hmmm. May I have the arrow and the sketch, Hagerup?"

After inspecting them carefully, he said, "The Snow Lemming, or *Dicrostonyx,* lives in the Arctic. His fur turns white in winter and he grows an extra claw for shoveling snow. Mother Nature has equipped the Snowmouse in much the same way. The shovel-shaped tail is for shoveling snow, and the white fur makes him invisible to his enemies. But note the Adorable Snowmouse's low brow, the small head. The brainbox must be tiny, unlike the large brain of today's civilized mouse. In my opinion he is a throwback to primitive cavemice, probably the last of his species!"

"Brilliant thinking!" said Hagerup. "And the arrow?"

Basil took scrapings from the shaft of the arrow, and studied them under the microscope before he spoke.

"No cavemouse made this! An arrow has four parts—the head, or pile, the body, or shaft, the nock, or notch, and the feathers, glued or tied to the shaft.

"Turkish mice made the finest arrows known.

The short feathers show this is of Turkish design, and it is inscribed with a quaint saying in Turkish, which I translate:

THIS ARROWHEAD WILL NEVER HIT A GOOD MOUSE

Hagerup and I leaned forward, keenly interested.

"Earth and grass scrapings prove the arrow was recently used. My dating methods tell me it is a year old. Yet I know of no arrowsmith today who could duplicate its beauty. Think back to the thirteenth century, my friends! A traveling Turkish arrowsmith, Byzant by name, visited Switzerland. He married, had four sons, and joined the dwellers in William Tell's cellar. A Byzant arrow was as finely crafted as a Stradivarius violin. The Tellmice appointed him Official Arrowsmith. And this arrow——"

We could hold back no longer. "You mean——"

"Precisely. This arrow was made by a descendant of Byzant! This arrow is the clue mice have sought for six centuries! This arrow may solve the Greatest Mystery in Mouse History—THE LOST COLONY!"